MOUNTAIN MAN'S OBSESSION

MEN OF MAPLE MOUNTAIN BOOK ONE

SADIE KING

MOUNTAIN MAN'S OBSESSION

MEN OF MAPLE MOUNTAIN BOOK ONE

His one obsession is her...

From the moment Colette sweeps into my bar, I can't stop watching her. Even when she doesn't know I'm looking. *Especially* then.

My cameras record her every smile, every frown, every moment. I study her until I know my girl inside out, my obsession growing, overwhelming me, demanding I act.

She'll never find out my secret, will she?

Mountain Man's Obsession features an OTT obsessed mountain man and the curvy innocent woman he claims as his own. It's high heat, oh so sweet, and always with a happily ever after.

The Men of Maple Mountain series is set in the world of the Maple Springs. Each book is a standalone but best enjoyed together.

1

BEAR

er fingers pause in their flight across the keyboard. She sits back, nibbling the tip of her thumb, a self-conscious gesture, unaware of me watching her.

She sits upright in the booth her chestnut hair hanging in loose waves under her headphones.

"I guess she doesn't like your choice of music," Kit, my best buddy, quips as he follows my gaze.

Dragging my eyes away from the beauty in the corner, I pull him a pint of strong ale and set it on the bar in front of him. "She's concentrating."

He takes a sip, his gaze resting on her a little longer than I'm comfortable with.

"I wonder what she's writing."

My body stiffens. I'm not happy that he's showing interest in my girl. Well, not technically my girl yet, but she will be.

I cut a look at my best buddy but his gaze has already left her. He sips his beer and scans the room. Either he knows she's mine, or he's not interested. Hopefully the latter. I'd hate to have to fight my best friend.

"Historical romance."

He gives me a pointed look. "You've spoken to her, then?"

That's not how I know what she's writing but I'm not going to tell him my secret.

"We've met. Her name's Colette."

The name swirls around my tongue and sends a shiver of longing through my body, my blood thumping in my ears.

My Colette.

To hide my reaction, I grab a tray of glasses from the dishwasher and start drying them. Kit gets the hint and drops the subject.

While I put the glasses away, Kit leans against the bar. Suddenly he sets his beer down and his eyes narrow.

"Who's that with your sister?"

I follow his gaze, and my chest tightens.

Ursula's seated at her usual table with her best friend, Heather. I served them low alcohol vodka in their cocktails, but they don't know that.

There are two guys at the table with them. One is leaning over Ursula with a leery look on his preppy boy face.

I know everyone of drinking age in Maple Falls, population 1,300-ish, and I don't recognize these kids. They're either up from Maple Springs for the night or tourists, here for the hiking trails.

Since my parents passed in a climbing accident eight years ago, I not only inherited the bar, but responsibility for my little sister as well. It was easier when she was still at school. But now she's twenty-two and just home from college, and every randy boy on the mountain is trying to get in her pants.

Not on my watch.

Slinging my dishcloth over my shoulder, I approach her table and cross my arms, so my muscles are on display alongside my tattoos. I fix my eyes on the skinny boy staring at my sister's tits.

"Evening, gentlemen."

My voice comes out as a low growl. I'm a big guy, six-foot-five and almost as wide as the mountain.

The kid jumps when he sees me and the leery look slides off his face.

Ursula looks like she wants to stab me in the eye. "Bear. What are you doing?"

"You know this guy?" the spotty kid stammers.

"He's my brother." Ursula rolls her eyes. "Here to protect my virtue."

"Can I see your ID?"

Kit comes up behind me, as if I need back up, but he's almost as protective of my sister as I am.

The boy fumbles in his pocket and shares a look with his friend.

"We, um left it in the car. I'll just go get it."

They scamper through the door and Kit follows, watching them all the way to the car park.

"Do you think they're coming back?" Heather asks wistfully.

"No," says Ursula. "Would you come back if this guy threatened you?" She gestures at me.

"You'll thank me for it one day, sis."

"When I die a lonely old maid?" She gives me a sarcastic smile, but her eyes are dancing, and I know I'm already forgiven. My sister's too smart to go for a gangly kid like that anyway.

Kit returns and I motion him over, putting my hand on his shoulder.

"Keep these ladies company would you, Kit? Make sure those young bucks don't come sniffing around again."

"Sure." He doesn't hesitate, which is why he's my best friend. Always willing to help out, even if it means babysitting my sister.

On my way back to the bar, I do the rounds clearing tables and talking to my regulars.

The Amery brothers are in town, Chase as chatty and good natured as his brother Rowan is surly and silent. Rowan's ex-military, and I give him a drink on the house whenever he's in town. Which isn't often. Doesn't like people much, that one.

The only person I don't chat with is Ewan, the recluse who never talks. He likes to sit on his own, staring at the mountain and sipping his whiskey. I can't imagine what demons he's wrestling with inside. But it's not my place to judge, only to serve.

His glass is empty, and I bring him another whiskey. Scotch, to go with his Scottish accent. He nods at me and silently raises his glass in thanks.

By the time I get around to Colette's booth, she's gone. There's an empty coffee mug and a napkin. On the napkin is a faint imprint of her lips, shiny and coffee stained, like she's pressed them to her lip-balm covered mouth.

Glancing around the bar to check no one's watching, I press the napkin to my own lips, right on the imprint. It smells like cherry lip balm and coffee, exactly how I imagine she'll taste when I finally kiss her.

Slipping the napkin in my pocket, I take the empty mug to the bar.

Later that night, the last punters finally go home, so I lock up and go upstairs to my apartment above the bar.

With eager fingers, I open my laptop and pull up the CCTV feed from the bar. The live feed shows it's all quiet downstairs, but that's not what I'm here to look at. I scroll back until I find the recordings from earlier tonight. Until I find Colette.

There's one CCTV camera trained on the bar, another one pointing outwards toward the door, and a third pointing to the left-hand side of the bar. Then there's the one I installed last week, after the first time she walked into Bear's Brewery.

She blew in with a flurry of autumn leaves, all five-foot-nothing and wrapped up in a red coat and matching knitted hat, her hair splayed out behind her. Her cheeks were rosy red, her eyes bright, and her beauty so surprising that the glass I was holding dropped right out of my hand. It shattered on the floor along with my heart.

She smiled at me and ordered a coffee then selected the booth in the corner, the one overlooking the mountain.

While I burnt the coffee and over-frothed the milk, she pulled out her laptop and put on a set of headphones.

For the first hour, she just stared at the mountain, letting her coffee go cold. It made me agitated, watching her. I wanted to know what she was doing, where she'd come from, but she was in such a reverie I didn't want to disturb her.

Then she began to type.

The next day, she came back and repeated the ritual in the same booth.

That night, I installed my fourth CCTV camera, above the booth. That's the feed I pull up now.

I've watched her every night since. Replaying the

feed, pausing and zooming in to see what she's writing, to catch her smile, to examine the lines of concentration on her face when she's thinking.

I know every expression, every turn of her mouth. I know the thumbnail on her right hand is worn down from nibbling it when she's thinking. I know she sometimes hums along to whatever music is in her headphones. I know she smiles along with her characters and mouths the words when she's writing dialogue.

There's no explanation for this obsession. I should talk to her, ask her out. But then I'd have no reason to watch her. And I like watching her.

She's so petite, but there's nothing petite about her curves. She must think I'm a brute with my height and bulk and rugged beard. Plus, she writes romance. I know this from reading her screen. What does a guy like me, raised on the mountain from a long line of mountain families, know about romance?

So, I watch, and I wait, looking for the right opportunity to show her we're meant to be together.

I scroll back to when she arrived today, pausing on her face as she stares out the window. There's a serenity to her, a peacefulness that's endearing.

Under her coat she wears a tight sweater. Her breasts are pushed against the fabric.

That's what catches my eye now – her tits straining to be let out.

I imagine them in my hand, caressing her nipples as I ravage her body.

Undoing my fly, I catch my dick in my hand. Thinking about her curvy body writhing under me, I thrust into my palm.

Remembering the napkin, I grab it from my pocket and press it against my nostrils, inhaling her scent. It's all I need to send me over the edge, shooting hot liquid into my palm.

Breathing hard, I set the napkin down alongside the other memorabilia I've collected.

One day, I'll talk to her, make her mine. But for now, I'm content to watch.

2

COLETTE

"*This ain't no place for a lady, Elizabeth.*" *His amber eyes sparked like fire.* "*I'll see you safely down the mountain.*"

Elizabeth picked up the hunting spear, still dripping crimson from the morning's catch.

"*You may as well spear me through the heart if you send me away.*"

My nose crinkles at the screen and I delete what I've just written. After a moment's thought, I try again.

"*A trapper's life ain't the life for a lady.*" *His amber eyes shimmered like the embers in the grate.*

"*I'll judge what life is best for me.*"

. . .

My fingers delete that too. I pull my headphones off and rest my head on my hands in frustration.

I came to Maple Falls to find inspiration but today I'm nothing but distracted – and by one big burly distraction in particular.

"Another coffee?"

The sound of Bear's voice makes me jump.

He grins sheepishly. "Sorry, I don't like to disturb you when you're working but, it looks like you might need a this."

"Thank you."

He holds out the cup like an offering and I gratefully accept.

Our fingers brush, sending a tremor of heat coursing through my veins. My hand wobbles and a dribble of coffee slips over the rim of the cup, pooling on the saucer.

Bear may not want to disturb me, but he sure is. The man exudes a pure animal magnetism.

Every time I lay eyes on him, my heart wobbles and my panties dampen. I tried staying away from the bar and writing in my rented cabin, but being away from him was even worse. I spent the whole day wondering what he was doing and who he was talking to.

He may think I'm sitting here working all day, but the truth is, I spend a lot of my time people watching, and when I say people, I mean Bear.

Even when he's not in my line of vision, I can hear the reassuring rumble of his deep voice through my headphones. The hairs on the back of my neck stand on end when he's clearing a table behind me. More than once, I've turned around and found him staring straight at me.

There's an attraction between us, for sure. I've written and read enough romance books to know that a pull like that can't be ignored. Sooner or later, the pull will get too strong and our bodies will collide. I'm waiting for him to make the move, and in the meantime, enjoying this delicious cat and mouse attraction.

It's been three weeks since I arrived in Maple Falls, the tiny town halfway up Maple Mountain. My new series is set in a small town in the 18th century with rugged mountain men who are trappers and hunters. Problem is, I grew up in California, on the beach with no idea what it's really like to live up a mountain. So, I decided to find out.

I found a cabin to rent and came for a week. That was three weeks ago. Once I saw the mountain, I knew I had to stay longer. Then I met Bear, the growly bar manager, as rugged as one of my characters.

In fact, as I've gotten into the story, when I write William, the hero, it's Bear that I think of. William has suddenly become very tall and wide and protective.

"How's the writing going?"

Bear seems genuinely interested, and I'm flattered that he's asking. But then, he's a bar manager, it's his business to talk to the clientele.

"Some days are better than others," I confess.

He nods sagely as if he knows what I mean. "Maybe you need a break."

He's probably right. I tend to go all-in when I'm working on a book. There are many long, frantic writing days, and I don't come up for air until the book is finished.

There's an old trapper cabin I've heard about that's a short hike up the mountain. Maybe tomorrow is a good day to take off from writing and go take a look.

"Do you know the abandoned trapper cabin in the mountain?" I ask.

Bear pulls on his beard, a long, luscious beard that I'm longing to run my hands through. "Which one?"

"There's more than one?"

"Oh yeah, the mountain's full of them. My great, great, great, great grandaddies on both sides used them."

My breath hitches. This guy really is the quintessential mountain man. It's in his blood. And there's something so attractive about that.

He opens his mouth like he's about to say something else when there's a shout from the bar.

"Can't a man get a beer around here?"

Bear spins around, his face like thunder. When he sees the large smiling man at the bar, his expression slackens. "Be with you in a minute, Colton."

He shrugs apologetically as he turns back to me. "That's my buddy Colton, he doesn't come down the mountain much. You'll have to excuse his manners."

He holds my gaze and I could get lost in his deep grey eyes, the same color as mountain stone.

"Hey!" Colton shouts again.

"Duty calls," Bear says, tearing his gaze away from mine.

He saunters over to the bar and claps his equally big friend on the shoulder. Their deep voices boom through the bar. But it's the rumble of Bear's voice that rolls through my body, causing a rush of heat between my legs.

Yeah, I definitely need a day off to cool off.

Pulling out my local guidebook, I find the page with trappers' cabins in the area. There's one about an hour's hike from town on a main walking trail. I circle it in the book before slipping it back in my bag.

3

BEAR

Sweat beads at the back of my neck and I undo a button of my shirt, letting cool air circulate. It's a warm day for autumn and Colette has set a steady pace. She's surprisingly nimble for someone of her stature. She's definitely petite in height only, there's nothing petite about her wide hips and heavy breasts.

My throat goes dry just thinking about her curvy body. Stopping behind a bush I quietly pull my water bottle out of my backpack and take a long cool drink.

She's a few feet ahead of me on the track and has no idea I'm here. When I saw her circle the cabin on this trail in her guidebook on the camera last night, there was no way I was going to let her walk all over the mountain on her own.

I could have invited myself along, and I almost did. But I get the sense it's a writer's thing, something she wants to do on her own. Maybe visit the place where her characters might have lived and let her imagination run wild.

She's probably got all sorts of visions going on in her head right now that I don't want to disturb.

Better to leave her alone with her own thoughts and not disrupt the creative process.

Besides, I enjoy watching her when she doesn't think anyone is around.

Humming reaches my ears from further up the trail, the sweetest sound that pierces right to my heart and causes me to grin like a maniac.

Colette continues to hum as she walks and sometimes breaks into song. Old country music mostly, sad and sweet.

Carefully stuffing my water bottle away, I shoulder my backpack and follow the humming.

A half-hour later we're at the old, abandoned trapper's cabin. It's a single room log cabin, tucked between ancient trees. The wood is dark from rot and the roof is caved in and coated in moss.

Not far away is a rock ledge and this is where I approach the clearing from, having cut into the trees a while back. I quietly slip behind the boulder stack as I watch Colette explore.

Her wide-eyed excitement is endearing; she's like a

kid in a toy shop, running her hand over the ancient wood and taking pictures.

A wood pigeon startles and flies out of a nest on the roof, squawking angrily. Colette squeals and pulls her hand to her chest. When she realizes it's a bird, she laughs at herself, a silverly peel that echoes through the forest and straight to my heart.

Carefully, so as not to make a sound, I climb the boulders and lie on my stomach at the top. From here, I have a good view of the area and can watch her as she takes photos and scribbles notes in her notebook.

She walks over to the boulders and I dip my head down, but she doesn't look upward. When I dare to peer over the edge again she's sitting below me, her back resting against the boulder.

She pulls her sweater off and I get a bird's eye view of her substantial cleavage.

As she gets a snack out of her backpack, I can see right down her top to the lacey edge of her bra.

Heat jolts through my veins and my blood thumps in my ears. My cock hardens instantly and my throat goes dry.

She sits back and her tits press together forming a perfect V. How I'd love to slide my cock between them, feel her soft tits around my hardness.

My breathing is so heavy I'm sure she must hear me. The pressure in my dick is unbearable as it presses into the rock. I have to move or I'm going to injure myself.

Sliding my legs around the boulder, I knock a pile of loose pebbles and they go cascading over the side.

Shit.

My body freezes, waiting to see what will happen.

The stones tumble to the ground landing right next to Colette. Any second now she's going to look up and see me lying here, watching her with a hard on like weird pervert.

I'm sprung.

Before she looks up, I slither quietly backward and then jump to my feet. Shouldering my backpack, an untucking my shirt so it hides the bulge in my pants, I walk to the edge of the rock, as if I've just gotten here.

"Hey," I say, as calmly as I can muster. "I wondered if I might find you here."

4

COLETTE

My neck swivels upward to the boulder above me, wondering what caused the mini rock fall. I shield my eyes from the sun and in the next instant, it's blocked out by an impressive figure. My breath catches in my chest when I realize it's Bear.

He's standing on the top of the boulder with his hiking gear and rugged beard, looking like he's just stepped out of the 18th century.

"Hi," I manage to squeak.

He scrambles down from the boulder and, standing beside me, is no less impressive.

"Good day for a hike."

He trains his pale eyes on me. My heart flutters in my chest and there's a pull in my belly that sets my core aching.

"You're not working today?"

"My sister's looking after the bar."

He sets his backpack next to mine and leans one shoulder casually against the boulder. It's the closest I've been to him and my knees feel giddy. I lean on the rocks for support.

"You here to see the cabin?"

"I want to see how the trappers lived." I remember that I mentioned it to him at the bar yesterday. Did he know I would be here, at this one? Then again, I guess it's the closet and the one most popular with tourists.

"What brought you up this way?"

"This is one of my favorite trails." He looks away when he says it and I get the odd feeling there's something he's not telling me. But what do I know about this man? He could be up here for any number of reasons.

"You must have been just behind me on the trail."

He pulls on his beard. "Yeah. Must have been."

He turns his gaze to me and takes me by the elbow. It's like a bolt of heat shooting through my arm and all the way down my body. I look up sharply, wondering if he felt it too.

His slate gray eyes give nothing away.

"I'll show you the cabin."

He leads me over to the shack in the trees.

"My great, great, great, great, great, great grandaddy Bear used to come up here and stay weeks at a time gathering and preparing skins to trade."

"Your ancestor was called Bear too?" I'm fascinated by this man, a piece of living history right in front of me. My skin tingles and I don't know if it's my writer's curiosity or something more.

"Oh yeah, family tradition. So was my dad and his dad before him. First son is always called Bear."

A vision pops into my head, a baby boy in my arms, a boy called Bear. Wow, I barely know this guy and I'm fantasizing about having his babies. My cheeks flush.

Stooping to get through the door frame, Bear enters the cabin. The floorboards are uneven and he holds his hand out, helping me inside.

He keeps my hand firmly tucked into his as my eyes adjust to the dark. When they do, a rusted metal cot frame is the only sign of human habitation. The floorboards are rotten and debris from the forest litters the place.

"There's not much here."

He squeezes my hand, sensing my disappointment.

"It's been abandoned a long time, and tourists have come through looking for souvenirs."

I look around the tiny cabin trying to imagine what life was like here. "There's not much space for a man to live."

He pulls at his beard, nodding. "Aye, it was a hard life for hard men. Ain't no place for a lady."

The line is from my book. I look up sharply.

Bear's studying the wall, running his hand over the wood. "Always lots of hooks in old cabins like these."

He seems completely oblivious to the fact he's just quoted a line from my book. And why wouldn't he be?

I just wrote it yesterday, there's no way he could have known. It must be a coincidence. I put the thought out of my mind.

"It must have been lonely for the men up here."

My arms go around myself and I shiver. I think of the men staying out here alone, no women for company.

"Most of them managed to find a woman eventually, or at least my ancestors did, or I wouldn't be here today."

He turns around suddenly and in the cramped space his body is so close we're almost touching. I feel the pure magnetism of him. This strong pull that emanates from my core.

"Let's get back out into the light. I can't see you properly in here."

He takes my hand again and we walk back to the boulder. My mind is in a whirl and my body is on high alert. This was supposed to be a break, a time for me to recharge. But with Bear around, I'm agitated, my body hot and flushed.

Pulling my water bottle from my backpack, I wrap my lips around the bottle and take a long, slow drink. When I lower the bottle, Bear is watching me.

His dusky grey eyes are fixed on my lips and he's breathing heavily. My pulse quickens.

I realize that I love his gaze on me, his intensity. I want him to keep watching me like that. My tongue flicks over my lips and I bite the lower one.

A low growl comes from Bear's throat that echoes through my body and rattles my bones. He closes the distance between us and his lips smash into mine.

White hot heat shoots through my body, and I feel his kiss all the way down to my toes. Bear's hands go around my waist and he lifts me up and sits me on a boulder so I'm on the level with him.

"Colette." My name rumbles off his lips sending a delicious shiver all the way through me.

"I've been wanting to kiss you ever since you walked into my bar."

He says it as his mouth crawls over my neck, his hot breath making every hair stand on end.

"I've wanted this too," I admit.

His mouth reaches mine and our tongues tangle, putting all the pent-up passion from the last few weeks into the kiss.

My legs straddle his waist and his presses in between them. There's a hard lump poking into my belly and I moan when I realize what it is.

Bear makes a deep grumbling sound. "You make that noise again, and I'll take you right here, right now, against this boulder."

His eyes are stormy and hooded, full of desire, and I believe what's he's saying.

I moan again.

"You're in trouble now."

He claws at my top, grabbing my left breast in his giant hand, rough and needy. I moan again and again and again as his hand slides to my shorts and he tugs at the fly. My pussy is on fire and I want this man with every nerve ending in my body.

Suddenly, there's the sound of a branch snapping and human voices. Bear pulls away from me, turning quickly and shielding my body.

I almost cry out at the loss of him. I'm aching for his touch and my hard nipples chafe against my top.

Then I see why he pulled away. Strolling into the clearing are a couple, hiking packs on and chatting amiably.

Trying to get my breathing under control, I scramble to do my shorts up and straighten my top.

"Hello!" the couple calls cheerily when they see us.

"Morning," says Bear in a low grumble that sounds like he wants to kill them.

I giggle, and he turns to me.

"You're lucky they turned up, or you were about to get ravaged right here."

I suck my lower lip, my body aching for what it just missed out on. "I don't feel lucky."

My eyes travel down his body and I giggle again.

"What's so funny?"

My head jerks pointedly at the stiff bulge protruding from Bear's khakis. "You might want to hide that or you'll scare the tourists."

He gives a sheepish grin and pulls his shirt over his waist.

"Come on," he says, helping me down from the rock. "Let's get back to town."

We hold hands on the hike down the mountain. It feels so right, so natural to have his big hand over mine.

He asks me to his place for dinner, but we both know what he means. We've got unfinished business. My body tingles in anticipation the whole way back.

5

BEAR

A few hours later, I'm stirring bolognaise sauce as I wait for Colette to arrive.

The trek down the mountain was a master class in self-restraint. Now that I've had a taste of Colette, my blood's running hot in my veins. I'm agitated and restless knowing I was so close to having her, to claiming her as mine.

I could have taken her into the bush and rutted like wild animals on the side of the mountain, but I restrained myself. The first time should be special. It should be on my bed with a soft pillow under her, not a hard rock.

There's a knock at the door and I turn the element off, giving the sauce a final stir. If I can make it through dinner without ravaging her, it will be a miracle.

My place has two entrances – the staircase at the back of the bar that leads straight to the living room and the outside entrance. She's used the latter, likely so no one at the bar sees her and gives her a hard time.

I open the door and my jaw hits the floor.

She's wearing a figure-hugging black dress that clings to every curve of her perfect body. My heartbeat thumps in my ears and my dick stands to attention.

All my resolve melts with one look at her body.

"Come in." My voice is low and growly.

I've been aching for her ever since I laid eyes on her, and since kissing her at the boulder today, I've been in a state of arousal that's blissful torture. Her body brushes past me as I shut the door behind her. It's too much.

"I like your place..." Her words turn to a squeak as I pull her toward me. My arm wraps around her waist and her hot, plump body is pressed against mine, sending sparks of desire coursing through my veins.

My mouth finds hers and she kisses me passionately, as hungry for this as I am.

"Colette." My mouth moves down her throat. "You're driving me crazy."

Her hips wiggle against me and I groan, my hard on straining painfully against my fly. Fuck waiting for a soft bed, I must have this woman – now.

My hands run over her soft rump, down her thighs, and to the hem of her skirt. Sliding up her thigh, my pulse races as I near her hot center. My hands slide over her soft inner thighs and straight to her soft, sticky mound. My fingers stop and I pull back to look at her. She bites her bottom lip, looking sheepish.

"You're not wearing underwear."

She giggles like a naughty schoolgirl. "I was going to tell you at dinner and watch you squirm."

"Oh honey, I can't wait till dinner."

Her breath grazes my throat, barely a whisper. "Neither can I,"

Her hands fumble at my fly and my pants drop to the floor. She gasps when she sees my thick cock sticking straight out and already dripping.

Her eyes are wide and she looks slightly terrified.

"Don't worry, honey. I'll get you good and warmed up first."

"Bear, there's something you need to know."

I freeze. This is where she tells me about the boyfriend back home or her husband or something. She bites her lower lip and looks away.

"What is it, honey?" I tilt her chin so her eyes meet mine.

"I'm a virgin."

Holy fuck. This just got ten times better. "You mean no one's been here before?" As I say it, I run my fingers over her soft pussy folds.

She shakes her head. "No one."

Not breaking eye contact, I slide a finger into her dripping entrance. "No one's ever been inside this sweet little cunt?"

My finger slides in and out slowly. Her eyes go wide

and she pants. When she speaks, it's a whimper. "No. I was saving myself."

I give her two fingers and she groans. "You were saving yourself for me, weren't you?"

She nods.

"Say it, honey."

Dark eyes, full of need, fix on me. "I was saving myself for you, Bear. Just for you."

My name is like honey on her lips. It speaks to something primal deep inside me. I growl as I capture her mouth, nipping at her lips while I finger fuck her, feeling her pussy suck me in. My palm rubs against her hard nub, making her squirm.

"It feels so good, Bear. Don't stop."

"I'm not gonna stop, honey, not until you come all over my fingers."

She moans, a high-pitched noise that makes my body tremble and my dick drip with longing. I slide another finger in.

"Oh god, Bear, something's happening."

"Don't fight it, honey, come for me."

She screams out my name as she shatters around me. Her pussy grips my fingers and releases a hot stickiness. I hold my hand inside her until she stops trembling, then slowly withdraw.

"That was amazing." She's breathing hard, her tits heaving up and down in her tight little dress.

"I'm not done yet, Colette."

I pull the dress over her head and drop it to the

floor. She's in nothing but her black lacey bra, the most gorgeous sight I've ever seen.

My cock throbs for her, and my whole body will explode if I don't get inside this woman. I grab her hips and lift her against the wall, spreading her legs open.

I imagined our first time in a bed, but I don't have time for that. I need her now.

"Hold on, honey."

She clings to me with her legs while I push her up against the wall, my dick finding her entrance.

My tip grazes her folds and even that contact is like an electric shock through my body.

Thoughts of taking it slow flee my mind. The animal inside me takes over and in one quick thrust, I impale her on my cock. She cries out, her nails biting into my back. I pull back, only to slam into her again.

"Bear!" She cries out and I pause, balancing her on the end of my dick.

"What is it honey, am I hurting you?"

"No, don't stop, it feels so good."

She's right. It feels fucking amazing. Her pussy tugs at my cock, sucking me in and wringing me out until I feel completely undone. Unable to control myself. I slam into her sweet cunt again and again, pulling her hips down so she rides my cock.

She's screaming my name, and the way she's loving it spurs me on till I'm in a fucking frenzy. She is mine, all mine.

Her screams get more high-pitched and her pussy

tugs at my cock as she orgasms again. It's too much, and I explode as well, shooting myself deep inside her and coating her walls with my seed until I've got nothing left to give.

She's taken all of me, all that I am.

Holding her close, I carry her into the bedroom. As I lay her down on my bed, I'm already getting hard again. The first time might not have been in a bed, but the second time will be.

Fuck dinner. I'm dining out on Colette tonight.

COLETTE

Two weeks later…

My fingers fly over the keys as I type the last scene of my book. I'm sitting on Bear's couch with my laptop balanced on my knees.

Since we hooked up two weeks ago, I've spent most of my time here. It's nice to write in the bar sometimes, but Bear is too much of a distraction. Whenever he's in the same room as me, my thoughts are scattered and my body longs for him.

At least up here I can focus on writing for a few hours a day.

My characters have found each other and, in the epilogue, they have a brood of mountain children. I try to come up with a name for a young girl character.

Looking for inspiration, I open an internet browser and type in *girls names western America 18th century*.

The round icon on the corner of the browser spins, but nothing comes up. That's odd. I try again and this time a message tells me I've got no internet connection.

It's a part of mountain life I'll have to get used to – dodgy internet connections. I smile at the thought. It's not being said yet, but I'm sure Bear and I feel the same. When my book's finished, there's no way I'm going back to California. My life is here now, with the big bear of a man I love.

Smiling to myself, I put my laptop aside and go over to Bear's desk in the corner to check if he has internet connection.

Opening his laptop, I bring up an internet browser. It does the same twirly button thing and I sigh in frustration. I'm closing the browser when something on the desktop catches my eye.

There's a folder titled "Colette".

My heart is in my throat as I click the icon, wondering what I'll find. The folder contains video files; I click one to start it playing.

It takes me a moment to realize what I'm looking at. It's the bar, but not just any part of the bar. This camera is trained on my favorite booth. And it's zoomed in on *me*.

My skin prickles and my belly clenches.

I open another video. It's me, writing at the bar on a different day. I try another one and another and another. They're all videos of me.

Sitting back with my heart racing, I put my trembling hands between my knees.

That's how he knew I was going to the cabin that day, that's how he knew the line from my book. Bear had been watching me, all this time. He engineered our whole relationship.

My mind is in a whirl, my skin prickly with heat and my chest constricted. Our whole relationship is based on a lie.

There are other folders on the desktop and with trembling fingers, I click through them to see the other CCTV feeds of the bar.

In one folder I find the live feed. It shows what's going on downstairs right now. Bear is at the bar drying a rack of glasses and talking to some customers.

I force myself to look at him hard. He looks happy, carefree, like the man I love, not some weird voyeur.

One of the men says something and Bear tilts his head back and laughs. I can imagine the sound, the deep rumble of his voice.

Just thinking about it makes my core melt and my panties dampen. I clamp my thighs together. I've just found out he's been watching me without my knowledge! I shouldn't be having this kind of reaction.

But the more I watch him, the wetter I get.

He dominates the bar with his big frame, confident and sturdy. One hand rests on the bar and I know that hand, I know what it's capable of doing. My nipples pebble and the heat between my legs becomes unbearable.

I slide a hand into my pants and palm my nerve center, needing some relief. One hand rubs myself while the other slides down my bra, teasing my nipple. All the time, I keep my eyes on Bear. He doesn't know I'm watching him and that makes it all the more thrilling.

He pours a beer for someone, his muscles flexing as he does it.

That's my man, I want to scream, my man.

My core explodes, and my pussy contracts, coming over my fingers. I squeeze my eyes shut tight as the orgasm races through me, feeling all its intensity. The way it shatters my body is delicious release.

When I open my eyes, I look to the screen. Bear's not there.

Leaning in, I scan the other feeds, trying to get a glimpse of him somewhere in the bar. Then I hear the door open.

7

BEAR

It's been two hours since I kissed Colette goodbye and headed downstairs to the bar. And that's two hours too long.

Ursula's just arrived, so I leave the bar in her hands and bound up the stairs to see my girl. I push open the door that leads straight into the living room and freeze.

She's sitting at my desk, my laptop open to the CCTV of the bar.

Shit.

I'm an idiot for not getting rid of the videos of her. I knew I should've deleted them, but every time I try, I can't bring myself too.

"I found the files." Her voice is husky and her cheeks are flushed.

"I can explain." I stride across the room and kneel in front of her. "I love you, baby. From the moment I saw you, I couldn't take my eyes of you."

She's breathing hard and I don't know if that means she's going to cry or scream or what.

"You're so fucking beautiful; I just want to watch you all day."

Fuck, this isn't coming out properly. I need to make her understand.

"You're my world, baby, you're my everything."

She's looking at me, her eyes dark and hooded, her chest heaving up and down. I wait for her to say something, knowing my whole future depends on her reaction.

Then she does something completely unexpected. She takes my hand, opens her thighs and presses my palm between her legs.

Her panties are dripping wet and I catch a strong musky scent, like she's juiced up and ready to go.

"Colette?"

I'm totally confused. Is my girl telling me it's all right?

"I found the files, and I found the live CCTV feed." As she speaks, she moves my hand over her wet pussy, rubbing herself against my palm.

I'm mesmerized by her intense look; my heart is in my throat and my dick's as hard as stone. If this is her way of telling me to fuck off, then it's pretty confusing.

She leans in and brushes my ear with her mouth, her warm breath making me shake.

"I watched you."

Holy fuck. "Do you mean..."

She moves her hips and slides them forward, rutting against my hand.

"It means I'm really fucking horny, Bear."

Holy crap.

She's pulling at my belt and my cock's out in an instant.

My girl knows I watch her, and she likes it. Holy fuck, I've hit the jack pot.

Pulling her out of the chair, I hitch up her skirt and tear her panties off. I lift her into the air and line my dick up with her hole.

"I fucking love you, Colette," I say as I slam into her. She bucks her hips, wriggling against me as I carry her to the couch.

Still inside her, I sit on the couch, keeping her impaled on my cock. She straddles me as I slide her up and down my length.

"I fucking love you," I chant with every thrust.

"I love you too, Bear."

It's the sweetest thing to hear with my cock buried in her. I take her over the edge then explode around her. The intensity of the orgasm makes me see stars.

Afterward, I pull her tight and kiss the top of her head.

"I like watching you, Colette. But if you want me to stop, I will."

She leans back and looks at me. "You don't have to stop, Bear. I think I like watching you too."

My heart soars. She gets me, she understands.

"You're perfect for me, honey. How about you stay here and be my mountain girl? We'll get married."

She squirms around so she can see me.

"Are you serious?"

"Of course," I growl. "You're mine and I want to make it official. What do you say?"

"Yes!" She throws her arms around my neck. "I say yes!"

Six years later…

The keyboard blurs as my fingers race over it. I'm working on my latest book, writing it in my favorite booth at Bear's Brewery.

The scene comes to an end and I sit back, sighing triumphantly.

Through the window the mountain looms, solid and dependable, and I catch my pale reflection in the glass.

I'm wearing a low-cut t-shirt and without looking at the CCTV camera on the beam overhead, I lean forward, letting my top fall open.

My breathing becomes shallow, knowing that later tonight, Bear will be watching this.

The bar's pretty empty for a Wednesday afternoon and I give a quick glance around. Bear's behind the bar talking to Kit, his rumbling voice like a beacon to my soul.

Slowly, so no one notices, I slide my hand down my top. Now I do look at the camera, giving it a long, sideways glance. I bite my lower lip and tilt my neck back as my hand runs around my nipple.

Before anyone sees, I pull my hand out of my top and slide it between my legs under the table.

That'll give Bear something to watch later.

Feeling pleased with myself – and horny as hell – I try to concentrate on the words in front of me.

It's been six years since I came to Maple Falls and I've never left. Mountain life suits me and as long as I'm with my mountain man, I'm happy.

The door of the bar opens and the sounds of children laughing make me spin around.

Bear jr runs in, the twins, Wolf and Coyote, toddling behind.

"They've been no trouble," Ursula calls to me.

Bear comes from behind the bar and scoops Coyote up in his arms. She squeals with delight, grabbing his big beard. A real daddy's girl, that one.

"Pizza, pizza," Chants Wolf.

"All right," Bear booms. "I'll get the pizzas going."

I close my laptop as my booth is invaded by little people.

Wolf puts his little hand in mine and crawls onto my lap and Coyote snuggles in next to me.

Bear comes to join us and the little ones all scoot over to make room.

"Did you have fun with Aunty Ursula?"

"We had ice cream," says Bear jr, grinning. One leg moves restlessly, kicking the booth. At almost six-years-old he's tall for his age and looks like he'll be as big as his daddy one day.

Smiling as my family surrounds me, I realize we're growing the next generation of the mountain. And I couldn't be happier.

Complete the Men of Maple Mountain series for your swoon worthy OTT alphas.

Each book is a standalone but best enjoyed in together.

Men of Maple Mountain

Mountain Man's Obsession – Colette & Bear

Mountain Man's Captive – Annie & Colton

Mountain Man's Virgin – Brooklyn & Chase

Mountain Man's Muse – Heather & Kane

Mountain Man's Redemption – Bethany & Ewan

Mountain Man's First Time – Ursula & Kit

Companion titles

Mountain Man's Healer - Jenny & Rowan

All the Scars we Cannot See - Emily & Sam

Boxset Collection

Men of Maple Mountain Books 1-7

Includes a bonus short story:

Mountain Man's Steamy Anniversary - (Bear & Colette)

PROTECTING HIS BRAT

This brat needs to be taught a lesson, and I'll be the one to discipline her...

Since retiring from the special forces, I've set up a team of elite personal security guards.

But I wasn't expecting the daughter of my first client to be such a brat.

Adrianna thinks she can play me, but she needs to be taught a lesson.

I'll be the one to take her over my knee.

She needs to learn that the only game I'm playing is for keeps.

Protecting His Brat is an OTT age-gap romance featuring an older military hero and a young curvy virgin.

Keep reading for an exclusive excerpt or visit:
mybook.to/ProtectingHisBrat

PROTECTING HIS BRAT

CHAPTER ONE

Bronn

It's an unusual house. Box-shaped rooms, jutting out at odd angles, looking like building blocks a child has stuck together.

The sun glints off the floor to ceiling windows, making me wince even behind my sunglasses.

It doesn't look homely, the hard lines making it look uncomfortable, unwelcoming, like a fortress. I should know. I've been staring at it all fucking day.

A black Mercedes waits on the driveway, the chauffeur as bored as I am.

But I'm good at waiting. I learned it in the Army, how to be still while remaining alert and how to spring into action when needed.

All good traits to be a security guard, which is about the only work I could find when I retired from the special forces.

Still, clients pay top dollar for ex-military, especially when you've been in the Green Berets.

Finally, the front door opens, and my client, Phillip Brooks, steps out.

His dark tailored suit contrasts with the sun gleaming off the white walls of the house. His wife stands in the doorway, twisting her hands nervously, looking at him with doleful eyes.

He slides an arm around her waist, and I look away as he embraces her. I feel a pang of regret. The military life never allowed me to settle down with a woman. I wonder what it's like to have someone to say goodbye to, someone to miss you when you're away.

He steps away, and she tugs on his sleeve, not wanting him to leave. Gently, he pries her hand off his arm and hurries down the stairs.

He stops next to me, and I get a whiff of bourbon and expensive aftershave.

"Don't let her leave the property."

I nod, letting him know I've understood his instructions.

My client explained the threat to me, the death threats he's been getting, his concern for his wife.

If someone had threatened my woman, I wouldn't be fucking off and leaving her alone. But it's not for me to judge. From what I understand, when you're in the oil business, like my client is, threats are a part of life.

The chauffeur holds the door open for my client, and he slides into the waiting car.

There's a wrought iron gate at the entrance to the property, and I scan the area around it, making sure there's nothing suspect before we open the gates.

As the car circles around the drive, I catch movement on the road.

My skin prickles, and I'm instantly on high alert. A black car is driving slowly down the road, too slow to be going straight past.

I jog in front of the Merc, holding my hand out to stop them. My client ducks down in the back seat, protecting himself from whatever threat this might be.

The black car comes to a stop outside the gate. It's got tinted windows, so I can't see who's inside.

Every fiber of my body is alert, my blood thumping, ready to meet the threat. I pull my piece and aim it at the car, keeping my hand steady.

The back door of the car opens, and I train my gun on whatever's going to come out of there. I won't be the first to fire, but if someone attacks, I won't hesitate to shoot.

There's the flutter of bright fabric, a flash of tanned leg, and a young woman slides out of the backseat. She's wearing a short, floaty dress that comes halfway up her thick thighs. It dips at the front, displaying a full cleavage of soft breast.

My mouth waters, and there's a twitch in my pants.

If this is how my clients' enemies attack, then I'm screwed.

She can't be a day over twenty, but my dick doesn't seem to mind the age gap.

The woman shuts the door behind her and saunters over to the gate.

She slides her large designer glasses down her nose and peers at me over the rim, unimpressed by the gun I've got pointed at her.

"If this is the welcome I get, I would have stayed away." Her voice is as pouty as her look. Sassy and sharp.

I've been trained to encounter all kinds of enemies but not an entitled brat with a sticky pink pout and a mane of golden hair clasping an overnight bag to her plus-sized chest.

A car door slams behind me.

"Put the gun down, Bronn."

I slowly lower my piece, but I can't tear my eyes away from the woman. She wraps both hands around the iron bars and leans forward rattling the gate.

"Open the gate, Daddy."

Her voice is whiny and petulant, like an overgrown toddler. Like a spoiled brat who needs some discipline.

My client strides forward, irritation in his voice. "You're supposed to be at college."

The woman tears one hand off the gate and swipes at her golden hair. "It was boring."

"Did you get kicked out?" My client's voice is clipped, his anger not quite disguised.

The woman gives him a sweet smile.

"I wanted to be here with you instead."

My client harumphs and pushes the code for the gate. It swings open, and the woman sashays through.

"I've got a business trip. You can stay here with your mother."

"Oh, great," mutters the woman, and even though I can't see behind her glasses, I'm sure she's rolling her eyes. If any kid of mine spoke about my wife like that, I'd tan their hide. But her father doesn't react.

"Don't give your mother any trouble," he barks at her. "I'll be back in ten days. You stay inside these gates and I'll deal with you when I get back."

The daughter does a slow twirl as if checking out her surroundings. Her eyes rest on me, and my body tenses as she looks me up and down.

"Who's the heavy?" she asks her father as if I'm not there.

"I'm Bronn."

Both the woman and her father look at me in surprise. To them, I'm the hired help, the silent security guard. But this brat needs to learn some respect. If her father isn't teaching her ,then I will.

She slides the sunglasses onto her head, showing off her large brown eyes. There's a mischievous look in them as she saunters toward me.

"Hello, Bronn."

My cock lengthens despite myself. I shift uncomfortably, clasping my hands in front of my body, hiding what's going on in my pants.

"I'm Adrianna."

From a distance, she was beautiful, but up close, she takes my breath away. I literally can't breathe as I stare at her, transfixed by her dark, playful eyes.

Heat sweeps over me, and I feel unbalanced. A surge of protectiveness rushes through me, and one thought bangs into my brain.

Mine.

"Bronn's here to protect you and your mother. Do exactly as he says and don't do anything stupid."

She's so close to me I can smell her cherry-flavored lip balm and expensive floral soap.

"Oh. I'll do exactly what you tell me to do," she murmurs so only I can hear.

My gaze flicks to her lips, so full, so pouty—just the right size for my cock.

Then she flicks her hair and flounces up the driveway.

I am so fucked.

Keep reading at: mybook.to/ProtectingHisBrat

GET YOUR FREE BOOK

Sign up to the Sadie King mailing list for a FREE book!

You'll be the first to hear about exclusive offers, bonus content and all the news from Sadie King.

To claim your free book visit:
www.authorsadieking.com/free

BOOKS BY SADIE KING

Maple Springs

Men of Maple Mountain

All the Single Dads

Candy's Café

Small Town Sisters

Sunset Coast

Sunset Security

Men of the Sea

Underground Crows MC

The Thief's Lover

Kings County

Kings of Fire

King's Cops

For a full list of titles check out the Sadie King website

www.authorsadieking.com

ABOUT THE AUTHOR

Sadie King is a USA Today Best Selling Author of short instalove romance.

She lives in New Zealand with her ex-military husband and raucous young son.

When she's not writing she loves catching waves with her son, running along the beach, and good wine, preferably drunk with a book in hand.

Keep in touch when you sign up for her newsletter. You'll even snag yourself a free short romance!
www.authorsadieking.com/free